MOUSEKIN'S
EASTER BASKET

MOUSEKIN'S EASTER BASKET

Story and Pictures by
EDNA MILLER

Prentice-Hall Books for Young Readers
A Division of Simon & Schuster, Inc.
New York

To Elsie and Jingles

Published by Prentice-Hall Books for Young Readers
A Division of Simon & Schuster, Inc.
Simon & Schuster Building
Rockefeller Center
1230 Avenue of the Americas
New York, NY 10020

10 9 8 7 6 5 4 3 2 1

Printed in Spain
Prentice-Hall Books for Young Readers
is a trademark of Simon & Schuster, Inc.

Library of Congress Cataloging-in-Publication Data
Miller, Edna
Mousekin's Easter Basket.
Summary: After a harsh winter, Mousekin's
springtime search for food brings him in contact
with brightly colored eggs, a white rabbit,
and other symbols of Easter.
1. Mice—Juvenile fiction. [1. Mice—Fiction.
2. Easter—Fiction] I. Title.
PZ10.3.M5817Mme 1986 [E] 86-22511
ISBN 0-13-604141-8

Mousekin listened as raindrops
pelted the forest floor.
The spring rain ran in rivulets
by moss-covered rocks and wildflowers.
It trickled its way along twisted roots
and down into Mousekin's
home in the ground.

When the first drops of rain splashed his coat
and dampened his leafy nest,
Mousekin raced up to the forest floor.
He knew he must find a new home soon:
one that was high and dry
and safe from sudden spring showers.

When the rain had stopped
and tree toads sang their nightly chorus,
Mousekin hopped outside.
The little mouse squeaked with surprise
when a large white furry creature
suddenly leaped past him
and disappeared into the forest.

More hungry than afraid,
Mousekin nibbled wildflowers
that grew at the base of the tree.
Only woodland creatures know
which plants can fill and which can kill.

As he nibbled and gnawed
he heard a thumping sound.
Then in a crash of underbrush
he saw a young fox run away.
What could have frightened
a hungry young fox who wanted
a mouse for its dinner?

Mousekin hurried to the top of the tree
and hid in its flowering branches.
When he recovered from his fright,
he spied a robin's nest.
It was just the right size
for a white-footed mouse
to make a snug new home.

As Mousekin scampered up to the nest,
the mother bird returned.
There were pale blue eggs in the little basket,
waiting to be hatched.
Mousekin ran back to the forest floor,
as the robin scolded him.

Not far from the tree, Mousekin could see
a nest built of twigs and grasses.
The towhee's nest was the right size too,
but built too close to the ground.
The mother bird called, "Cheewink, Cheewink,"
as she guarded her pink-speckled eggs.

Mousekin heard another sound—
a rapid thumping on the ground
that he had heard before.
It warned Mousekin of danger near.
It startled a weasel who couldn't decide
between pink-speckled eggs
or a mouse for its dinner.

Just as the weasel sprang away
Mousekin spun about to see
a HUGE white rabbit.

Its long furry ears
were lined with pink.
Its eyes were pink-colored too.
A torn and tattered ribbon
hung loose about its neck.

The rabbit was bigger than a snowshoe hare
that turns to white in winter.
Much bigger than a cottontail,
but Mousekin was not afraid.
A rabbit wouldn't harm a mouse.
Rabbits eat grass and wildflowers, too.

When Mousekin hurried on his way
to find a safe new home,
the big white rabbit followed after.
The creature was lost in the forest
and afraid to be alone.

Mousekin explored many trees in the woods.
He discovered many nests.
Some were filled with pale tinted eggs
and others with newly hatched chicks.

When Mousekin returned to the forest floor,
after his search in a tree,
he felt safe from dangers on the ground
for the big rabbit sat waiting for him.

Mousekin knew he must find a home
before the day was done.
It isn't safe for a white-footed mouse
to be up and about with the sun.

High on the branch of a wild cherry tree
Mousekin discovered a nest.
It was empty and safely hidden
beneath a leafy umbrella.

The little mouse made many trips
from the top of the tree to the floor below.
He gathered moss and grasses
to build a mouse-sized shelter
inside the robin's nest.

Mousekin was so busy he didn't stop to see
that the big white rabbit had run off to a clearing
and was romping with cottontails.

A long-eared owl saw the rabbits at play.
It saw a white-footed mouse at work.
There were hungry young owls in a far-off nest
waiting to be fed.

Mousekin waited until daybreak
before he looked about.
Red tulips and yellow daffodils
were growing everywhere.
They were not like any flower
Mousekin had seen in the woods,
and the strong, sweet scent of hyacinth
made his whiskers twitch.

From his perch in the evergreens,
Mousekin spied a large nest on the ground.
The brightly woven basket
was filled with large colored eggs
unlike any he had seen before.
Some had dots and some had stripes.
They were a rainbow of color.

Just as Mousekin hurried down
to peek inside the basket,
his big white rabbit friend
poked her head through the branches.
She wore a bright new shiny ribbon
about her furry neck.

In that same instant a small hand reached in
and snatched up the egg-filled basket.
"We found them! We found them!"
he heard small children shout.
Mousekin darted from his hiding place
and raced back into the forest.

When Mousekin stopped to nibble some flowers,
he heard the rabbit's thumping sound;
the rapid drum of its hind foot on the ground.
It warned him again of danger.
Looking about, he caught sight of the owl,
as it swooped down into the clearing.

The big white rabbit and the cottontails
leaped in all directions.
When Mousekin heard a rabbit scream,
he fled away in terror.
He ran 'til he came to the edge of the woods
and dove into a thicket of green.
He waited for the rabbit to follow,
but his pink-eyed friend never came.

He hurried to his own little nest
high in the cherry tree branches.
Just before Mousekin curled up to sleep,
a robin heard him singing.
His high soft chirps and trilling sounds
were as sweet as any bird's.